Monkeys and Dog Days

Kate Banks
Pictures by **Tomek Bogacki**

Frances Foster Books
Farrar, Straus and Giroux New York

To the brothers I know –K.B.
For Tadzio –T.B.

Distributed in Canada by Douglas & McIntyre Ltd.
Color separations by Chroma Graphics PTE Ltd.
Printed and bound in China by South China Printing Co. Ltd.
Designed by Irene Metaxatos
First edition, 2008
1 3 5 7 9 10 8 6 4 2

www.fsgkidsbooks.com

Library of Congress Cataloging-in-Publication Data
Banks, Kate, date.
Monkeys and dog days / Kate Banks ; pictures by Tomek Bogacki.— 1st ed.
p. cm.
Summary: When Max and Pete get a new dog, they learn that taking care of a pet is not as easy as they thought.
ISBN-13: 978-0-374-35029-1
ISBN-10: 0-374-35029-9
[1. Dogs—Fiction. 2. Pets—Fiction. 3. Brothers—Fiction.] I. Bogacki, Tomasz, ill. II. Title.

PZ7.B22594 Mo 2008
[E]—dc22

2007060726

Contents

A Real Dog

Max's father was busy doing yard work.

"Would someone get me the wheelbarrow?" he asked.

"Dad needs the wheelbarrow, Max," said Pete.

Pete was Max's older brother. He was playing Frisbee with a friend.

Suddenly the Frisbee sailed onto the neighbor's lawn.

"Would you get that, Max?" said Pete.

"Just because I'm the youngest in the family doesn't mean I have to do everything for everyone," said Max.

Max got the Frisbee and tossed it back to Pete.

Then he sat down on the steps and began talking out loud.

"Who are you talking to?" asked Pete.

"Rufus," said Max. "He's my dog."

"You don't have a dog," said Pete.

"Yes I do," said Max.

"Not a real dog," said Pete.

Max cuddled his imaginary friend. "If you put your hand out, Rufus will shake your paw," he said to Pete.

Pete put his hand out. He shook his head. "What we need is a real dog," he said. "A real dog is good company. A real dog is fun."

"A real dog is a lot of work," said Mom. "You can't just imagine cleaning up after it. You have to actually do it."

"We can do it," said Max.

"Easy," said Pete. "We're good workers."

Max got the mop and began cleaning the kitchen floor.

Pete set the table.

After dinner, Max cleared the dishes and Pete put them in the dishwasher.

The next day, Dad came home with a surprise.

"Is it a dog?" asked Max.

"No," said Dad. "It's a book about dogs."

"We can look at it together," said Mom.

"Oh," moaned Pete.

Max opened the book. He turned to the first chapter: "Showing Your Dog Who's Boss."

Pete read aloud. "'It's important to let your dog know who the leader is. If he doesn't learn, he will try to be the leader. Then he may seem pushy and disobedient.'"

Max read next. "'Dogs need food, exercise, and love.' Just like people," he said.

"That's right," said Dad.

Pete continued reading. "It says here that a full-grown dog has forty-two teeth, which need to be brushed at least once a week."

"That'll be my job," said Max.

"Hey," said Max. "It says dogs sweat through the pads of their feet. I didn't know that."

Mom turned to the last chapter. It was her turn to read aloud.

Dogs get big.

Dogs bark a lot.

Dogs chew things.

"Are you still sure you want a dog?" asked Dad.

"Yes," said Max. Pete nodded and turned to the final page of the book. "'If you give a dog what he needs, you will have a friend for life,'" he read.

Family Fudge

Mom and Dad drove Max and Pete to the animal shelter.

"We'd like a dog," Pete said to the young woman who was in charge. Her name was Maggie.

"We have quite a few dogs who need homes," said Maggie.

"I think we can take just one," said Max.

"That's fine," said Maggie. "But we want it to be the right one."

Maggie gave them a form to fill out. There were questions about their home. Was it in the country or the city?

There were questions about the family. How many people? What were their ages?

"Good," said Maggie. She brought out the first dog for them to meet.

"Too big," said Mom.

The second dog was lively. It jumped onto Max playfully.

"Too rambunctious," said Dad.

The third dog wandered up to Pete. He lay down and closed his eyes.

"Too sleepy," said Pete.

But the fourth dog was perfect. She trotted right up to Max and waited to be petted.

"Hi," said Max.

Pete rolled a ball to the dog, and she rolled it back.

"Good dog," said Pete.

Then the dog wandered over to Dad and licked his shoe.

"She's cute," said Max.

"Does she have a name?" Mom asked.

"She's called Fudge," said Maggie.

"Welcome to the family, Fudge," said Dad.

Fudge had a big appetite. Puppies need to eat three times a day.

Max measured out her dog chow. Fudge always wanted more. Max shook his head sadly. It was hard to say no to someone you loved.

It was Pete's job to make sure Fudge had plenty of water in her bowl.

Fudge loved to play. She batted the tennis ball with her left paw.

"She's left-handed," said Max. He'd read that dogs were either left-handed or right-handed, just like people. Max was left-handed.

Every day, Max and Pete brushed Fudge. When she got dirty, they gave her a bath.

Fudge splashed a lot.

“The book didn’t say we’d end up cleaning the whole bathroom when we gave our dog a bath,” said Max, wiping down the walls.

Dad built Fudge a doghouse. Max put a soft pillow inside.

"Come on, Fudge," said Max. But Fudge didn't want to sleep in the doghouse.

"Now I know where the expression 'in the doghouse' comes from," said Pete. "Not even dogs want to be in the doghouse."

Fudge preferred the big house.

She listened eagerly outside the door when Pete and Max had their music lessons.

She nuzzled them when they gave her a biscuit.

She licked their faces when they felt sad.

Dog Do and Dog Don't

Fudge grew quickly. She was a smart dog. She learned to fetch, to sit, to roll, and to shake hands. Max always gave Fudge a treat or said "Good dog" when Fudge did something well.

She became housebroken, too. But she still needed exercise. Pete and Max took turns walking Fudge.

One day, it was Pete's turn. But he wanted to play with a friend. "You walk Fudge," he said to Max. "My feet hurt."

Max put Fudge on her leash and led her down the driveway. "Don't your feet ever hurt?" he said to the dog. Then he remembered that dogs had padded feet.

Fudge was hungry after her walk. "It's your turn to feed the dog," Max said to Pete.

"Okay," said Pete, but he forgot. He was busy repairing the tail of his kite.

Max fed Fudge. Then Fudge rolled in some fresh mud, and Max gave her a bath.

"Good dog," he said.

Fudge stretched out to dry in the sun.

"I don't know where the expression 'It's a dog's life' comes from," said Max. "This dog's life is pretty good."

Pretty soon Max was doing all the work. "That's what I get for being the little guy," said Max.

Fudge brushed up against Max's leg and licked his face.

Max threw Fudge a stick. "Fetch," he said. Fudge got the stick and brought it back to Max.

"It looks to me like you're the big guy," said Max's father.

Take Me to Your Leader

The hot, sticky days of summer set in. It was July.

“These are what they call the dog days,” said Max’s father.

“Why is that?” asked Pete.

“This is the period when Sirius, the dog star, rises with the sun. It’s the brightest star in the sky. People used to think Sirius was responsible for all this summer heat.”

“Speaking of heat,” said Max, “Fudge needs her water changed.” He’d read that dogs don’t like their water too warm or too cold. It needs to be just right.

“You do it,” said Pete. “I’m late to the park.” He gave Fudge a quick pat on the head and raced off. He took Fudge’s ball with him. Fudge barked loudly.

"Never mind," said Max. He poured Fudge fresh water and walked her into the shade. Fudge lay down for a nap with her paws in Max's lap.

That evening, when it cooled off, Dad mowed the lawn. "What's this?" he said. Fudge had pooped in the garden, and no one had scooped it up.

"Clean it up, Pete," said Dad. "I believe it's your turn."

"I can't," said Pete. He was lying on the sofa. He'd had a hard day at the park. "I'm exhausted."

"I'll clean it up," said Max.

The next afternoon, Pete's friends left for summer camp. Pete was alone.

"You want to play, Fudge?" he said, tossing the dog a twig. "Fetch."

Fudge did not fetch.

"Sit," said Pete.

But Fudge stood up on her hind legs.

Then she walked over to the tree and pooped.

Pete got the tennis ball and tossed it. Fudge ran after it. But she brought the ball back to Max.

Max gave Fudge a pat on the back. “Good dog,” he said.

"Hey, why is Fudge doing everything Max says?" asked Pete.

"Because Max does everything for Fudge," said Mom. "Dogs are loyal to their masters. And it looks to me like Max is the master here."

Pete's face fell. Max felt sorry for his brother.

He crouched down beside Fudge and whispered in her ear. "Go play ball with Pete," he said. And he held out a tasty dog biscuit.

Pete threw the ball.

Fudge was off after it. She brought it back to Pete.

"Good dog," said Pete.

That evening, Pete fed Fudge. He changed her water. And he brushed her.

He even helped Max pick up his room.

"Good brother," said Max, laughing.

Pete laughed, too.

"Woof," barked Fudge. And she wagged her tail happily.